Praise for Storyshares

"One of the brightest innovators and game-changers in the education industry."
— Forbes

"Your success in applying research-validated practices to promote literacy serves as a valuable model for other organizations seeking to create evidence-based literacy programs."　　　　　　— Library of Congress

"We need powerful social and educational innovation, and Storyshares is breaking new ground. The organization addresses critical problems facing our students and teachers. I am excited about the strategies it brings to the collective work of making sure every student has an equal chance in life."
— Teach For America

"It's the perfect idea. There's really nothing like this. I mean, wow, this will be a wonderful experience for young people."　　　　— Andrea Davis Pinkney,
Executive Director, Scholastic

"Reading for meaning opens opportunities for a lifetime of learning. Providing emerging readers with engaging texts that are designed to offer both challenges and support for each individual will improve their lives for years to come. Storyshares is a wonderful start."
— David Rose, Co-founder of CAST & UDL

Do You Think It'll Make a Difference?

Storyshares presents

Published by Storyshares, LLC
Inspiring reading with a new kind of book.

Storyshares
Storyshares, LLC
24 N. Bryn Mawr Avenue #340
Bryn Mawr, Pennsylvania 19010-3304
www.storyshares.org

Interest Level: Post-High School
Grade Level Equivalent: 5.1

ISBN 9798885977869
Book design by Saskia Globig

Do You Think It'll Make a Difference?

Rebecca Watson

Storyshares

Contents

Hour One

I awake to the shrill sounds of my alarm clock, an invasive and unwanted ringing in my ears. 6:30 am. I wince at the intrusion and keep my eyes closed for a while after. I enjoy the darkness and the quiet behind my eyelids, blocking out the world beyond them.

It's 7 am when I finally open my eyes and tune into the sounds of my family outside the door. There's the opening and closing of my oldest child's closet and the happy burbling of my youngest. I blink slowly and groan as I pull myself out of bed, with my feet landing on the wood-textured linoleum.

Squinting between the curtains my wife must have opened, I see that fog sits heavily on the ground outside. Dew clings to the blades of grass in my backyard, which is littered with various children's toys. I see a slightly muddy patch with tiny green soldiers scattered around, confidently holding their plastic rifles.

My eyes stop there for a moment. My concentration is finally snapped away when my bedroom door opens. I turn and see my wife, already dressed and ready for the day. Her halo of blonde hair frames her bright and smiling face.

"Oh, you're up!" she says in a surprised tone. "Good morning, I was just coming to check if you were awake."

"Yes, I'm awake. I was just about to get ready," I say tiredly, rubbing my face with both of my hands.

"Okay, breakfast is in about half an hour, so don't take too long," she says.

"I won't," I promise.

"Attaboy," she says with a wink, before leaving the room and clicking the door softly behind her.

I smile at where my wife stood, even after she has left and closed the door.

Heading to my wardrobe, I open the doors and push through the racks of clothes. I get to the suit section and take out my favorite one. As I pull it off the railing, something falls out of the pocket and lands at my feet. I lean down and pick it up, flipping it between my fingers.

Upon further inspection, I find that it's a few pamphlets that are folded up within themselves. I unfold them in my hands and read the printed text on them.

Your son next? is written in an offensive and bold black text, above a stark cross gravestone with a helmet resting on it. It's printed on brown paper.

The other says *If this mother and child were not American would you care?* on white paper with purple abstract line art. It shows an embrace between two figures, with sadness practically spilling off of the paper.

I hold the paper between my fingers. The sensation is somehow overwhelming to my senses. In the corner of my eye, I see the trash can just by the doorway inside the bathroom. It's empty and almost inviting me to hide something.

My eyes flick up to the shelf just above eye level in my wardrobe. It's piled high with articles, reports, and books, stacked and bookmarked in no particular order.

I quickly put the papers back in the pocket where I found them, careful not to bend them, but sure to hide them.

Still there, but currently unnoticeable.

Hour Two

The droning of the television set chokes out the morning news, with the regularly scheduled showing of violent videos and images.

A normal Thursday morning.

Sunlight fights through the fog, allowing a creamy glow to come in through the windows. It falls over half of the wooden table and the brightly colored tiles that my wife carefully chose and continues to maintain.

My wife, Marie, and daughter, Rosie, are sitting in the light. Their identical heads of blonde hair are bright in the frosty glow. Rosie waves her spoon around above her bowl of cereal, giggling every time the metal connects with the china and makes a noise. Marie simply watches with a happy smile on her face.

Thomas sits beside me on the darker half of the table, eating his breakfast with an unusual silence. His eyes are glued to the television. I place a newspaper clipping from yesterday beside my plate and begin to cut up my food.

My eye is caught by the images and voices coming from the screen behind my wife.

"Last month, thousands gathered at North Carolina State University to protest against the war in Vietnam, and they are expected to again later this week—"

The screen is filled with images of bell-bottomed and peace sign-carrying teenagers and young adults. They're waving banners with an almost religious ferocity, shouting and yelling their outrage and objections. I move my eyes back to my plate and take my first mouthful.

"How brave of them," my wife sighs, her face bathed in the sunlight as she smiles affectionately toward the screen.

"Brave in what way?" I ask.

"Standing up for what they believe in. It's admirable," she answers. She takes a sip of her coffee and leans toward the table to spear a piece of bacon with her fork.

"It's not that I don't agree with them, I just can't see what changes they are making," I say with a disappointed sigh, before taking a mouthful. "I just feel it is a waste of time."

"Maybe." She shrugs passively and takes her bite, but still watches the screen with a slight sparkle in the corner of her eye.

Rosie begins to fuss, forcing Marie to divide her attention and give her a small, metal car. Rosie makes engine noises as she pushes it along the edge of the table.

The report on the television changes to a helicopter emerging from the clouds, landing in a meadow in a wooded area. It spills out a stream of soldiers. Some are fumbling with their guns as if they don't yet know how to hold them. The others are moving them smoothly, as if they were a fifth limb.

I can't help but notice the boys' faces, lined with dirt and fear. Sweat clings to their fingertips and slips around the handles of their oversized weapons.

"Must we watch this so early in the morning?" I ask, dropping my fork and knife on the edges of my plate with a loud clatter.

My wife jumps slightly at my sudden out-

burst, and I realize the volume that I didn't care
to contain.

"We can turn it off. I only put it on because
Thomas asked," she says, with a hurt expression.
Her mouth creases at the corners slightly and a
furrow between her brows begins to deepen.

"Really?" I look over to my son beside me,
suddenly not so interested in the screen.

"There's no harm in keeping up to date,"
he says with a shrug. His eyes are downcast, with
curly brown hair falling over his forehead, much
like mine used to when I was his age.

"Read my articles if you care so much," I
say flatly, flicking open the morning paper that was
rolled up in front of my plate.

Weather, protests, civil unrest, sports...

"I would if they weren't so boring," he says,
almost whispering.

"Thomas! You cannot say things like that to
your father. Apologize," Marie says in a harsh tone.
It's different from her usual gentleness.

Thomas stays silent.

"What do you find so boring about my articles, son?" I ask, putting down my fork to meet my
son's annoyed look.

I move my eyes away from his and gesture
for my wife to turn off the television. She stands

up, not before giving me a pleading look, and turns off the television with a click. The room that was filled with the faint noise of reporting and gunfire is now filled with a crackling quiet, the silence almost deafening.

"Never mind. Sorry," Thomas says.

"That's what I thought," I answer, giving my wife a thin-pressed smile.

She answers with a roll of her eyes and sits back down in her chair with her arms crossed.

I just can't win this morning.

I finish my plate and pick up the morning newspaper, *The Washington Post*, that my wife had laid out for me. I do try to read it, but the writing style is so frustrating. These kinds of articles jabbing at the anti-war movement make me want to quit my job, they're such terrible wastes of paper. I may not want to participate in it myself, but I sure as hell would prefer protest over the alternative.

In the corner of my eye, my gaze is caught by the article clipping I had brought in with me. I'd kept it on my bedside table since I first read it yesterday afternoon. I sigh and lazily fold the over-sized embarrassment of a newspaper in half and drop it on the table. I unfold the clipping, running my fingers along the well-worn fold lines as I begin to read.

William L Calley Jr., 26 years old, is a mild-mannered, boyish-looking Vietnam combat veteran with the nickname "Rusty." The Army is completing an investigation of charges that he deliberately murdered at least 109 Vietnamese civilians in a search-and-destroy mission in March 1968 in a Viet Cong stronghold known as "Pinkville."

Calley has formally been charged with six specifications of mass murder. Each specification cites a number of dead, adding up to the 109 total—

"James?" I vaguely hear.

"Hm?" I pull myself out of my trance, returning to the world of my kitchen. I feel my eyes still twitching to look back down as I try to drag them away from the unfinished sentence I had been reading.

Well, rereading.

"I asked if you wanted more coffee," Marie asks gently, in her eternally patient tone.

—and charges that Calley did "with premeditation murder...Oriental human beings, whose names and sex are unknown, by shooting them with a rifle."

"Oh, sorry, honey, I was reading. Yes, please," I say after my pause to read.

I smile up to her while folding up the article clipping into a few more squares than necessary.

Enough that the words that are visible can no longer be strung together into those brutal sentences.

"You work too much." Her perceptive eyes look at the words beside my thumb, scanning over the sentence: carrying out orders.

"Have you been sleeping enough?" she asks with an intake of breath. She rests a hand on the side of my head and runs her fingers through my hair.

"Probably not," I admit.

She rolls her eyes disapprovingly, but still brushes a thumb along the side of my cheek. I smile up at her appreciatively, just briefly enjoying the moment.

"So I was talking to Joe the other day," Tom begins to say.

"Oh, honey, every time you talk to that Joe character you start saying the most ridiculous things," Marie says with a sigh.

Her hand drops away from my face and rests on my shoulder while she pours coffee into my mug. The contact allows me a sigh of relief, my anxiety lessening.

"Thank you, and your mother is right. That friend of yours is bad news," I say with a frown. I pick up my coffee and take a sip, looking my son up and down.

"Why'd you say that?" he asks. His face sours as he grips his fork in his fist, knuckles flushing white.

"First, it was that concert in August he wanted to take you to... What was it, Woodstock? Then it was the car project with the—" I begin, with a deep breath.

"Car!" My daughter giggles in a carefree manner, bashing a toy car into her cereal bowl with a smile.

"Oh, no," Marie whines, pacing to the other side of the table. She wipes the milk off Rosie's face and coos at her soothingly.

"My point stands. I don't like Joe." I turn my eyes away from my wife and daughter and look at my son.

His body is tense, his knee bouncing under the table and his eyes looking down at his breakfast plate.

"He's got good ideas sometimes..." Tom says.

"Such as?" I ask.

"A job for after high school," he answers, uncertain.

Well, that gets my attention.

"What kind of job?" I ask cynically.

I take another sip and readjust my position in my chair to face him. The wood of the chair legs drags against the tiles in the quiet of the kitchen.

"The kind with good money and lots of benefits and... team building skills," Tom says.

I place my mug down carefully and swallow harshly. My eyes briefly move to the now dark, but still warm, television set.

"James—" I hear my wife say, in a soft tone.

"Now, what kind of job has that kind of benefits right out of high school with no qualifications, son?" I ask. I ignore my wife and measure my voice to stay calm.

"Sure does sound like a great deal, but there must be downsides to such an attractive prospect, no?" I go on, with a tilt of my head and a snap in my voice.

I can feel a nervousness rising in my chest, just like my reaction to the news on the television and in the newspapers and—

"The Marines," Tom says, finally meeting me with a steely glare in his eyes and a defiant grit to his jaw.

"Absolutely not," I say.

"Dad—" Tom starts to say.

"You know how I feel about this. Absolutely not," I repeat.

He freezes at my reaction, and I realize just how loudly I said that. I make a conscious effort to calm my voice, but the tension in my voice remains.

"I find it uncomfortable enough to have to read and write about it at work, let alone allow my son to be involved in such a situation," I say harshly.

As I watch his body language, I realize he is simply waiting for me to finish talking. It just makes the anxiety inside me build to a boiling point.

"I avoid this war as much as I can, because I truly hate it, and I will most definitely avoid my family being affected by it," I finish at a louder volume. My voice wavers in the last sentence with barely controlled anger.

Tom's mouth twists like he can taste his unspoken words stuck in his throat. It is so similar to my own frown, whenever I have lost an argument I should have won or had a story unfairly stolen from under me.

"I didn't realize it was so bad—" Tom says.

"I've said it before and I'll say it again. You would benefit from reading some of my articles sometimes. Ralph does column upon column about the war, more than I would like if I am being entirely honest," I say.

My nervousness fades and my voice quiets at his apologetic tone. I pick up my newspaper and start reading again to avoid his or my wife's accusatory looks.

"What do you think I should do after high school, then, if you think you know everything?" Tom asks, an argumentative tone creeping back into his voice.

"Anything but fighting the Viet Cong, Tom," I sigh with finality before looking at his face. It is stormy and creased, frustration dug deep within the furrow between his eyebrows.

"I can see if I can get you a job at your grandfather's garage, how about that? Or you could go to college?" I ask helpfully, but the damage is already done.

I straighten out the newspaper in front of my face to block my view of him, ending the conversation. I hear his sigh from his half of the table, and the clatter of his fork on his plate. A scrape of his chair and the soft padding of his feet against the floor, and he's left the room.

"James," Marie says. "You could have been nicer."

"Marie, the war is brutal and horrific and there is nothing to be nice about in relation to it. I stand by what I said," I say.

"It's not that I don't agree with you on that, but he's scared. Don't you remember what it was like when you were 16, 17?" she asks, in a disapproving tone.

I shrug in passive agreement, turning to the sports page. In the silence, I turn the corner of my paper down to look at her.

Marie is sitting next to Rosie with a spoonful of cereal still hovering in the air near her mouth. Rosie sits with her mouth open, waiting for a spoon that is yet to come. But my wife's eyes are glued to the front page, moving back and forth as she reads the headline. I close the sports page and flip the paper over in my hands to look at the front cover page that I had not read.

I skim it briefly. Dozens dead, communists coming out of the trees and young American soldiers massacred. The regular headlines.

"You could have some sympathy, you know," she says softly, shaking her head as I move the paper.

She finally spoons the last mouthful of cereal into my daughter's mouth. Rosie claps her little hands together and jumps in her chair.

"For who? The Viet Cong? The brainwashed American soldiers? Goddamn Nixon?" I ask in frustration, closing my newspaper.

I go back to eating my breakfast, scraping eggs and bacon onto my fork and shoveling them into my mouth. Marie's eyes are still on the paper on the table, so I shift it under my plate out of view and wait for her answer.

"Any of them," she says, disappointment heavy in her tone.

I frown and tilt my head in confusion, but before I can question it, she takes my daughter out of her chair and carries her out of the room.

I am left alone in my kitchen, fork and knife in hand as I look out of the window. A crease grows between my eyebrows, and the glaring, frosty rays of sunlight shine on my table.

Hour Three

As I step onto my front porch with my briefcase in hand, I turn, hoping to see my wife. Usually she would wave me away with a smile on her face, but right now she is nowhere to be seen. I sigh in defeat and close the door behind me.

I slip the folded up article into my pocket. My fingertips brush against the other two pieces of paper.

I shove the newspaper under my arm to be able to hold my car keys. I walk down my front pathway, careful not to step on the beautifully-cared-for flower beds when I make my way to my 1965 Chevy Impala.

I get into my car, going to toss my paper and briefcase in the seat to my right. I grumble with annoyance as I see interior design magazines on the front passenger seat. I move them to the back seat to make space, and finally my hands are free. I turn on the ignition and smile at the comforting purr of my engine, pulling out of my driveway onto the street and switching on my radio.

"Good morning, Washington DC! It is a cold November morning, with high fog cover and a temperature of about 40 degrees, and here is the news. Last night in South Vietnam below the 17th parallel—"

I can feel the paper digging into my stomach from inside my pocket. I wince and pull the corner of my jacket so the pocket sits at my hip. I readjust myself and change gears as I switch lanes to pull onto the highway.

I use my free hand to turn to different radio stations. The radio crackles as I twist the tuner, the murmur of mumbled words as I try to tune into one.

"Nixon has—"

Not that one.

"Casualties have—"

Not that one, either.

I know I need to know a lot about the war, especially when I spend all my days editing articles about it. But that starts when I walk through the office doors. I avoid it as much as possible before that point. Well, I *usually* do...

I take the pamphlets and the article clipping out of my pocket, suddenly hyperaware of their presence. I place them on top of my newspaper, allowing the radio to crackle without my tuning.

I return my eyes to the road, focusing on the boxy red back of a Ford Mustang in front of me and the crunch of my radio. But I can still feel them in the corner of my eye: the purple line art, the black gravestone. Without taking my eyes off the road, I tuck the scraps under my newspaper. That's better.

I heave a sigh of relief, releasing a breath that I hadn't realized I was holding onto.

I go to tune my radio again, finally landing on a station that doesn't seem to be spewing an exhausting program of fearmongering. The back end of a song that I've heard before trickles off, with the fading of the guitars and a soul style of singing.

"Wow, what a great tune from Three Dog Night, their hit song 'Eli's Coming' at number 10 on the billboard hot 100. Next up, we've got a song highly requested by our younger listeners, so this one's for you guys!"

I hear the opening of drums, and of a

twangy guitar riff, building up to a vocalist singing.

I prefer the British ones. The Beatles, I think they're called.

I keep my eyes on the car's fender in front of me, turning up the radio. I gently tap my fingers along the top of my steering wheel, curled around like I'm scared someone will see. It's a popular song; it's not a crime to like it.

My mind strays back to my son, the defiance in his eyes and the insistence in his voice. The words of my wife ring true in my ears: "Don't you remember what it was like when you were 16, 17?"

Suddenly, that emotion in his eyes looks less like defiance and more like fear. A fear that I see in my own eyes more often than not when I look at myself in the mirror. I've managed to avoid thinking about this for a while now.

I'm too old to be drafted, and my son was young enough that I could avoid it up to this point. But with his 18th birthday months away, the draft lottery looms over my mind like a heavy cloud. But never in my wildest dreams could I imagine that he would want to enlist rather than be drafted.

It's practically suicide.

Does he know that?

I don't notice when "Fortunate Son" has finished. I don't even notice when a few songs have passed. I barely even register when The Beatles start playing, my mind still blank with fear. I really only shake myself back to reality when I'm parked in my spot in front of a small office building with a sign above it that says *The Washington Daily*.

Hour Four

I push the thoughts to the back of my mind. Right now, I have to walk into that office and be Mr. Miller for the day.

I squint through the fog and look at the front windows of my office. I can see all of the people I work with already at their desks. They are leaning down to look at their typewriters, diligently typing away.

I guess that's one of the perks of being Editor-in-Chief. I get to come in later.

I pull my briefcase off the passenger seat, tightening my grip and flexing my fingers around the wooden handle. I put my newspaper under my arm, but when I pull my briefcase off the seat to get out of the car, the pamphlets and newspaper clipping slip out. I sigh, not looking at them when I swipe them up in my hand and slip them in my pocket. I can't make eye contact with their accusatory messages.

I open the door of my car and step out, clearing my throat and bracing myself against the cold, winter air. I pull my coat closer around me before turning to lock my car and walking quickly to my office building.

I pull open the front door of the office, smiling at the warm air against my face and nodding to Barbara at the front desk.

"Good morning, Mr. Miller!" she says brightly, giving me a toothy, wrinkly smile. Her big head of curly brown and gray hair bounces slightly as she stands up.

"Good morning, Barb. How are you doing this morning, sweetheart?" I ask.

"I'm good, Mr. Miller. I've got your call list for today," she says.

She picks up her notepad of paper and follows me around the side of the reception desk. I take off my coat and pass it back to her, rubbing my hands together to warm up my fingers again.

"Thank you very much," I say, pushing the door open with my shoulder.

"Morning, Miller," Ralph grumbles from the an-
cient coffee machine, where he's pouring Scott a mug.

"Morning, Ralph," I say.

Scott raises his (now full) mug to me.

"Scott." I nod to him, looking to the rest of
the room.

"Good morning, Debbie." I smile at the woman
at the desk closest to me. "Have we heard back from
Marlboro?" I ask hopefully.

She's chewing on a cookie and holding a mug
of half-drunk coffee, but she covers her mouth and
gives me a thumbs up. She swallows to speak. "For
good money, too," she says.

"And this is why you're head of advertising."
I give her a wink and walk past her desk.

I give the rest of the room a wave. Half of
them greet me, half of them still have their heads
down, typing.

"If you've got anything interesting for the day,
come see me in my office now. But if it's the usual,
I want drafts on my desk after lunch," I say.

The room murmurs with understanding. Barbara
is still following me, her notepad still clutched in her
hand and my coat still resting over her arm.

"Here's your call list, and I'll go get your coffee,"
Barbara says loudly, setting the papers down on the
desk in front of my typewriter.

As she's closing the door behind her, she whispers, "And your morning cigarette."

"You're a doll." I give her a wink, and gesture for her to close the door behind her. When she does, my office is filled with relative quiet, with only the light hum of the working chatter out in the main room.

I place my briefcase on the floor and my newspaper on my desk beside my call list. I breathe a sigh of relief. I'm just pulling the article scrap from my pocket when I hear a few short knocks on my door.

In a panic, I shove it back into my pocket at the same time Ralph opens the door. He's wearing a sweater vest and corduroy trousers, with his hair falling around his face. He holds his cup of coffee and his usual notes for his brief.

"If you bring me another protest—" I start to say.

"I have prisoners of war." He cuts me off, moving to close the door.

"Wait, hold the door!" Barbara says, coming around the corner. She's holding my usual coffee mug in one hand and a packet of cigarettes in the other.

"Thanks," I say. I take them and she leaves the room again.

"You want one?" I ask Ralph, putting a cigarette between my lips and taking an ashtray out of my drawer.

"As long as you don't tell my wife," Ralph answers, and I laugh.

He opens the window behind me and takes one from the packet. He takes the lighter out of the same drawer where I keep my ashtray and lights his cigarette.

"So, are they interesting prisoners of war?" I ask, lighting my own and taking a long drag.

"Well, there's 928 of them, so there must be a few," he answers cynically, passing me his outline.

"Sure, run it," I say.

I see the edge of the newspaper clipping, which catches my attention.

"Unless you have something more interesting?" I say hopefully. I put the mug down on my desk and take another drag from my cigarette as I pick up the clipping.

"I might. But I'm not sure yet, I need to talk to Scott and see if he has anything on it," he says, taking a seat on my couch.

I take a deep sip, and his cheeks tighten with what I know is his thinking face.

"Did you read the *St. Louis Daily* yesterday?" he asks carefully.

In answer, I unfold the article and hold it up for him to read. "I did, and I had a feeling you'd like it." I smile at him, skimming over the top few lines again.

"Do you think we can get Barb to call him up? We could use that Hersh guy at one of our desks," he jokes. I shrug, but he goes on. "But in all seriousness, I think we could run something on it. I asked Scott to find something yesterday. I was gonna catch up with him after I spoke to you."

"Ralph, you know I'm the only one who can ask Scott to go find stuff. It all goes through me," I say tiredly, stubbing out my cigarette and drinking my coffee.

"Would it make you happier if I called Scott in here right now and he did have something, so I could have it on your desk after lunch?" he asks cockily.

I pause, thinking about my answer.

"You know I can't say no to that," I sigh, waving at him to stand up.

He grins at me excitedly, walking quickly to the door. He takes his cigarette out of his mouth and holds it behind his back when he leans around the corner to speak in the direction of Scott's desk.

"Scott!" he hisses.

I hear a sigh and the scrape of a chair against the floor. The thin reporter comes around the corner, pushing his glasses up his nose and juggling a small mountain of papers.

"Is this about My Lai?" he asks.

Ralph nods and gestures for Scott to sit on the couch beside him. He takes his cigarette from behind his back and takes a drag.

"Well, it all checks out," Scott says, taking a deep breath and flicking through some of his papers. "There are more interviews we could run with his army buddies, and there's definitely a bit more digging I could do."

Ralph looks at some of the papers and tosses the top one to me.

"We need to get on this, Jim; this is gonna be huge," he says, nodding to the note.

At the top, there is a date.

18 months ago.

The slaughter of innocent civilians happened 18 months ago, and we're just finding out about this now.

"There must have been a cover-up," I say, rereading the date. I can't believe my eyes.

"Oh, yeah. A huge one, at that," Scott says, passing me neater pages typed up with paragraphs upon paragraphs.

I skim-read them, words jumping out to me about generals and investigations and a huge amount of covering up by the government.

"Some say they were just following orders,

but what some of them were doing could never be conveyed in a set of instructions," Scott says darkly, pushing his glasses up his nose.

Ralph skims one of the pages. "This was a gluttony," he chokes out, passing me the paper.

On the page are bullet points of confirmed incidents at the scene of the crime, things that should never be summed up in a matter of lines.

"Rape, murder, torture, the killings of unarmed women, children, and old men, with no VC confirmed in the area. 'Gluttony' would be an accurate way to put it, if you think that some of these guys were hungry for murder," Scott adds, ticking off the crimes on his fingers.

"This isn't just bad, this is..." I trail off. I look through a few of the pages, totally overwhelmed by what I'm reading.

"War crimes. Geneva, Nuremberg. I was looking it up; it's practically fascist, Jim," Ralph says passionately.

Scott takes a sip of his coffee, raising his eyebrows at me in agreement.

"Okay, okay, I see your point," I say. "But we can't just print a column calling the US government a fascist military state filled with uncontrollable killing machines. One of us would get assassinated!"

Scott chokes on his coffee.

"You've seen what's been going on down south. And you can see how much of this is covered up. This is just what we know now; imagine how much more is gonna come out. And imagine what happens to us when it does," I say, holding up the pile of notepapers. "We've got to be careful."

"Okay... Look, Jim, I see your point. I won't call them fascists. But we've got to call them something; it's immoral if we don't," Ralph insists, pointing at the papers.

"Immoral? We're just reporters," I say, dropping them with disgust onto my desk.

"I'm not one to tell you what to write, not at all. I just find the information," Scott says. "But this went on all day. The soldiers who didn't want to do it? This guy, Calley, took their guns out of their hands, Jim. He shot the civilians himself."

It's jarring sometimes to remember that horrible things happen in Vietnam. I see so many pictures of the tall forests and the beautiful landscape of mountains and trails, so different from what I am used to. It feels a little bit morbid to try to appreciate the place when you remember it's practically covered in blood.

But at this moment, it is not so distant, not such a far-off place. Some of those boys with guns were scared, with sweaty hands and faces lined with dirt and fear, committing atrocities my mind can't begin to understand. Some of those men were enjoying the disgusting filth of their own immorality, their own monstrosity. Yet all of those people they killed were so scared and so helpless.

In the scared, inexperienced young soldier, I see my son as he is, eyes filled with fear. In the victims, I see my wife, so bright and breakable. In the murderer, Lt. Calley... I also see my son, grown to be angry and inhuman.

"He chased and shot down children, Miller. We've got to tell the world. It's our duty as humans, let alone reporters," Ralph adds quietly.

That last sentence hits me at my core.

All I can imagine is a blonde little girl, stand-ing as high as my knee, being chased—no, hunted down—by a man who holds a gun like he would never let go of it. In the corner of my eye, I see the stark purple lettering from the pamphlet I brought with me this morning.

If this mother and child were not American would you care?

There's another knock on the door, cutting through the silence that had blown up and filled the room at those last words spoken. No one dares to speak, but Scott sighs deeply and leans over to open the door.

Barbara is standing in the doorway, holding an opened envelope with what looks like pictures inside it. There's a short, handwritten note in her hand. Tears are dribbling down her cheeks.

Hour Five

"Barbara? What's wrong?" I ask with concern.

She chokes out another sob and leans across my desk, passing me the note and envelope. She puts a hand over her mouth before rubbing the stream of tears down her face.

Ralph leans back in his chair, crossing his arms with his eyes darting between us. The tension in the room only builds. Scott nervously shuffles the papers he has in his hand, lining up the edges so he's holding a thick brick of paper.

I flip the envelope over, my hands shaking slightly.

Barbara is so sturdy, but so positive. I've

never seen her cry before.

The front is addressed to the newspaper office building, but has an extra message scrawled on the front.

For the eyes of Editor-in-Chief James Miller only.

"Barb," I say, looking up at her with disappointment.

At this point she's dabbing at her eyes with a tissue, and Scott is holding a freshly opened packet.

"I know, I know! But we get letters addressed like that all the time. But that, that I can't—"

Crying a fresh gush of tears, she's unable to finish her sentence. She waves at me, wiping her face before leaving the room and shutting the door behind her.

The room is once again quiet, aside from the sound of Barbara blowing her nose. It's getting quieter as she walks back to her desk.

"Jesus, what's in it?" Ralph asks. He cracks his knuckles and looks out of the half-blind-covered window and into the main room.

"How would I know?" I ask, rereading the sender's name.

Ron Haeberle.

"Do we know a Ron Haeberle?" I ask.

Ralph rubs a hand over his face before shrugging.

"I might have seen some of his stuff before, just

a run-of-the-mill army photographer, I think,"
Scott says.

I read the note.

*These photos were taken on March 16, 1968,
in My Lai, Vietnam, documenting the actions taken
by American GIs from the Charlie company while on
a "routine" search and destroy mission. These were
taken on a personal, non-Army-issue camera while
I was deployed and have been sent to a number of
other newspapers. I urge you to publish them.*

Scott and Ralph look at me expectantly,
waiting for me to say something. Ralph is leaned
forward, watching my face while I read. Scott is
squinting at the white border and tiny slip of color
peeking out of the envelope in my hand.

I open the envelope and pull out the top picture, passing the note to Scott without taking my
eyes off the picture.

The first shows a field with long, thin grass
fronds and a helicopter in the foreground. Tall,
finger-like trees reach for the sky in the back-
ground. Men are captured in the act of jumping
out of the helicopters, running across the middle
of the picture. Not too bad. I pin the picture
between my pinkie and ring finger to look at the
next one.

The second is a similar image, with no helicopter but about five soldiers walking across a field, frowning and tense.

The third is a dirt road, with...

I lean closer to the picture.

Three bodies, lying flat on their backs, spaced out. As if they had run.

The fourth, another road.

But it's not three, or five, or ten. For as long as I can stand to look at the picture, I see at least a dozen bodies. Men. Women. Children. Young children.

The slaughter seems to have been random.

I keep flipping through the pictures, panic building in my chest.

The burning of houses, the stealing of belongings, people begging and pleading for their lives in the face of the evil before them.

A child, holding another child, lying huddled in the middle of a road. Alone and hurt. One seems to be alive in the photo, but I have no doubt it didn't survive the night.

"Damn," I finally say.

I toss the photos down on my desk, leaving the white envelope on top of them like I can hide from their reality. I push away from my desk and stand to look out the window, facing away from

Ralph and Scott as I blink the tears out of my eyes.

I take a deep breath and a cigarette from the packet, along with the lighter.

I hear the scuffle of papers and the sound of the thicker, heavier paper of the photos being picked up and flipped through. Two shuffles in, I hear a sharp intake of breath. I light the cigarette between my lips and take a deep breath, eyes on the trees in the skyline outside the office.

They're tall and finger-like.

"What should we do?" Scott asks, his voice wavering and unsure.

"We're running the story," I say. "Saturday edition, front page, get as much as we can out there." I take a deep drag of my cigarette, calmly turning around and piling up Scott's papers with military precision. "You'll need these when you start writing. You have the rest of the week to finish it," I say.

I pass as many of the papers to Ralph as I can hold in my free hand before sitting down heavily in my desk chair and spinning to face the window again.

"Really?" Ralph asks, almost excitedly.

"Really," I answer, not bothering to look at him.

I let out a puff of smoke, watching the tendrils curl in the sunlight from the window. The light sharpens. I watch the clouds above the trees drift across the sky. They show the piercing, cold blue of the winter sky with the light shining down on me.

"Do you think it'll make a difference?" I ask him.

"Definitely," he says, before leaving.

He closes the door behind him and leaves me in the fresh sunlight coming from between the parted clouds.

About the Author

Rebecca Watson is a 19-year-old amateur writer from Surrey, England. She is studying her Law LLB at Cardiff University, after studying History, English and Geography for her A Levels. Through her historical studies, she wanted to use historical fiction to give a more humanized perspective on history. In her spare time when she's not glued to a keyboard, she likes going on long walks with a book and a coffee flask through Bute Park and past Cardiff Castle, scrapbooking, and reading as many books as her bartending jobs can pay for.

About the Publisher

Storyshares is a publisher focused on supporting the millions of teens and adults who struggle with reading by creating a new shelf in the library specifically for them. The ever-growing collection features content that is compelling and culturally relevant for teens and adults, yet still readable at a range of lower reading levels.

Storyshares generates content by engaging deeply with writers, bringing together a community to create this new kind of book. With more intriguing and approachable stories to choose from, the teens and adults who have fallen behind are improving their skills and beginning to discover the joy of reading.
For more information, visit storyshares.org.

Easy to Read. Hard to Put Down.

www.ingramcontent.com/pod-product-compliance
Lightning Source LLC
Chambersburg PA
CBHW071226170626
46809CB00005BA/1954